For Carl[illegible]

Warrior Kids:

Not Just for Kicks

Mark Robson

24 June 2015

by

Mark Robson

First published in Great Britain in 2014
by Caboodle Books Ltd

A Catalogue record for this book is available from the British Library.

ISBN 978 0 9929389 1 8

Cover and Illustrations by Chie Kutsuwada
Page Layout by Highlight Type Bureau Ltd
Printed by CPI Group (UK) Ltd, Croydon, CR04YY

The paper and board used in the paperback by Caboodle Books Ltd are natural recyclable products made from wood grown in sustainable forests. The manufacturing processes conform to the environmental regulations of the country of origin.

Caboodle Books Ltd
Riversdale, 8 Rivock Avenue, Steeton, BD20 6SA
www.authorsabroad.com

For World Master, Jackson White, 7th Degree Black Belt, instructor, mentor and friend.

And for all those children who have come along and roared with me at Daventry Tigers – this series is very much for you. No matter how far you get along the tae kwon-do journey, I pray that you will live out your lives remembering the 5 tenets we have taught you: courtesy, integrity, self-control, perseverance and indomitable spirit.

Acknowledgements:

This series would not have been possible to write without the inspiration of all those who have encouraged my continued interest in martial arts. I won't name names for fear of leaving someone out, but you know who you are!

Also by Mark Robson

<u>The Darkweaver Legacy Series:</u>

Forging of the Sword

Trail of the Huntress

First Sword

The Chosen One

<u>The Imperial Trilogy:</u>

Imperial Spy

Imperial Assassin

Imperial Traitor

<u>Dragon Orb</u>

Firestorm

Shadow

Longfang

Aurora

<u>The Devil's Triangle</u>

The Devil's Triangle

Eye of the Storm

Contents

Chapter 1 – Chased

'Run, posh boy, run! Come on, lads. Don't let him get away!'

Donovan Richards didn't look back. He didn't dare. Leaping over the wall and into the park, he dodged through the bushes and out into the open. He could hear them behind him. It sounded like they were gaining.

Fear drove him. Gritting his teeth, he pumped his arms and legs, racing across the grass towards the woods at the far side of the park. Every panting breath burned his throat and his lungs felt like balloons so full of air that they were ready to explode at any moment. He'd never been a good runner, but he was determined not to let Zach catch him.

With a bounding leap, he hurdled the flower bed next to the path. He stumbled as he landed, but somehow stayed on his feet. The sound of the boys landing behind him sent his mind into a spinning panic. They were close – really close.

He tried to weave as he ran. It was a mistake. Before he realised what was happening, his feet were hooked out from under him. He was down, rolling over and over on the grass. Something in his school bag jabbed him in the back making him gasp with pain. A moment of pure terror was replaced by the cold sinking realisation that he could not escape. As he sat up he looked slowly round. Four pairs of legs in grey school trousers surrounded him.

Zach arrived, puffing like a steam train. His stocky body was even less suited to running than Donovan's skinny one.

'Well done, lads!' Zach panted, his eyes gleaming with nasty pleasure as he looked down at their captive. 'Let's take him... for a little walk... in the woods... shall we?'

Two pairs of hands grabbed Donovan's arms and lifted him to his feet. 'What are you going to do to me?' he asked, unable to hide the fear in his voice.

'You'll see, posh boy,' Zach jeered. 'Bring him, lads.'

This wasn't the first time Donovan had moved to a new area and a new school, but having to start afresh at the beginning of year six had never promised to be easy. From the moment Donovan had started at Oxtree Primary School at the beginning of the week the other kids had warned him to stay away from Zach and his gang. He'd tried, but it seemed being the new boy had attracted Zach's attention and the bullying had started before the first day was over.

To start with it had been the 'accidental' shoulder

barges in the corridor and the teasing about his 'posh' accent. But it had got rapidly worse. As soon as the other children in his class realised Zach was picking on him, they all stopped talking to him. None of them was willing to risk drawing the attention of Zach and his gang and within a few days Donovan was feeling isolated and lonely. The only person who showed any sign of wanting to be his friend was the other class outcast, a slightly chubby boy called Gurveer, and being seen with him felt like admitting defeat.

Donovan twisted his head left and right, hoping to see someone that he could call out to for help. There was no one about. He was going to have to face the five boys alone. For a moment he considered wrenching himself loose and making another run for freedom, but he realised that this was just wishful thinking. The boys holding him were bigger, stronger and faster than he was.

He felt powerless. Weak. Pathetic. Dread at the thought of what was about to happen began to grow inside him like a vine, coiling through his stomach, twisting and squeezing his gut. He felt sick.

Perhaps if I puke, they'll back off, he thought.

He didn't have time to find out. They were among the trees now, sticks crackling and crunching underfoot.

'Check his pockets!' Zach ordered. 'I'll do his bag.'

Hands rummaged through his pockets, digging right to the bottom. His school backpack was pulled from his shoulders and he was thrown to the ground at the base of a tree. Pushing himself hard against the trunk, he backed as far from the boys as he could.

Zach held out a hand and the boys put the contents of his pockets into it. He tossed the neatly folded handkerchief away and stirred through the remaining items.

'One pound sixty? I thought you'd have more cash than that, Donovan. You got any more hidden somewhere in this bag?'

Donovan didn't answer. He stared at Zach, a fiery anger building inside him. Was that what this was all about? Did Zach just want to steal his money? Now the boys had got what they wanted, would they leave him alone? The bully was going through Donovan's bag now, tossing the exercise books over his shoulder, scattering the contents of the pencil case and deliberately snapping the plastic ruler in two.

'No sweets. No money. No nothin',' Zach growled. 'That's a shame, posh boy. If you'd had anything worth taking, I might have left it at that. Now I'm going to have to find something else to make all that running worth the effort. Lift him, lads.'

The boys dragged Donovan to his feet again and without warning Zach punched him hard in the stomach. All the air rushed from his lungs and he folded, gasping for breath. Before he realised what Zach was doing, he felt a burning sensation between his legs as he was all but lifted from the ground by his underpants in a savage wedgie.

The boys around him roared with laughter as he folded to the ground, tears streaking his cheeks.

'Make sure you have more money on you next time, posh boy,' Zach growled. 'If you don't, we'll make things much worse for you, won't we lads?'

There was another round of laughter and Donovan heard the retreating footsteps and chuckling as the group moved away. It was over – for now.

* * * * *

'Master?'

'Driss! What kept you?' The Master's deep voice sounded cold as ice. 'Come in. I have a job for you.'

Driss did as he was told, but stayed as close to the door as he could without appearing impolite. Being in this man's presence made him tense. Some people found the tanks of venomous snakes, the dim lighting, and the almost tropical heat of the room uncomfortable. For Driss however, it was not the snakes, the light or the heat, but the human who made him nervous.

It wasn't the man's size, for he was no bigger or smaller than most men. Neither was it the man's strange behaviour or his insistence on the title *Master*, for Driss had met and worked for unusual people before. There was something cold and reptilian about this man. He was almost more snake-like than the cobras he kept. In the half-light of the large office his dark eyes looked dead and soulless like those of his pets, and his low voice was strangely hypnotic. Wherever Driss saw him, the Master was in shadowy surroundings and always wearing dark clothes. It was creepy.

Driss watched as his employer gathered some vials and placed them carefully into slots inside a wooden box.

'Take these to the laboratory, Driss,' he ordered. 'We're close now. I can feel it.''Yes, Master.'

'And Driss...'

'Yes, Master?'

'Any signs of trouble?' he asked.

'No, Master,' Driss answered, inwardly glad that he was able to say this confidently. 'As far as I know nothing is amiss.'

'Excellent! Excellent!' The Master took his place behind his desk and interlocked his fingers in front of his chin. 'All is proceeding perfectly.'

Chapter 2 – Karate Kid

Donovan didn't pause as he pushed through the front door. Kicking his shoes off on to the mat, he headed straight for the stairs.

'Hi, Donovan, honey! Good day at school?' his mother called from the kitchen.

'OK I s'pose, Mum,' he called back, determined not to let her know the truth. If his mother found out he was being bullied, he would be dragged down to the school in a flash to see the Head, and when the other kids found out he'd *never* hear the last of it. It was bad enough being the new kid in town. The last thing he needed was to have the other kids thinking he hid behind his mum at the first sign of trouble. 'Going to my room for a bit. Got some homework.'

'Tea will be in about half an hour.'

'All right, Mum.'

Donovan leapt up the stairs two at a time, turned right at the top and heaved a sigh of relief as he reached the haven of his room. With the door shut behind him, he dumped his backpack, dived on to his bed and grabbed the TV remote. He pressed the

power button and then immediately pressed and held the reduce volume button, dropping the sound to a whisper. His Mum would be quick to come looking to see why he wasn't doing his homework if she heard it, but the last thing he felt like doing right now was maths.

As the screen sprang into life, Donovan's breath caught in his throat. It was like he was watching his encounter with Zach and his gang all over again. There was a small boy being cornered by a gang of bigger boys who looked set on beating him up. What he'd done to upset them wasn't clear, but it looked very much like he was about to beaten to a pulp.

Suddenly, a new figure entered the scene. It was Jackie Chan. Donovan felt his heart leap in his chest.

'And where were you today when I needed you, Jackie?' he muttered, and then he smiled. Wouldn't that have been something?

If he fights like he did in the film The Spy Next Door, *and* Around the World in Eighty Days, *the bullies will get a taste of their own medicine now,* he thought.

Sure enough, the boys turned on Chan's character and, despite being outnumbered by the youths, he made short work of showing them they had picked on the wrong person. As the bullies ran away, the programme was interrupted by an advert break and Donovan rested his head back down on his pillow.

If only I could fight like Jackie Chan, he thought, closing his eyes and trying to picture what it would be like to have amazing martial arts skills. *I'd show Zach and his crew a thing or two then.* He tried to imagine himself as a whirling human tornado, arms and legs dealing stunning blows to Zach and the other boys. But no matter how hard he tried, he could not seem to fit his face to the super-human person in his mind. Who was he trying to fool? He was reminded of a joke about the best martial artist in the world who decided to join the army, but who accidently killed himself the first time he had to salute a passing officer.

Donovan smiled to himself. *That's more likely to be me,* he thought. *I'd probably injure myself rather than anyone else.*

The film resumed and Zach noted the title – The Karate Kid. He'd heard of it, of course, but not seen it before. He watched as Jackie Chan took the boy home and began to train him. The exercises looked hard, but the boy had a look of determination about him that made Donovan's mind begin to spin with questions. Was learning martial arts something he could do? The boy in the film was clearly fitter than he was, but fitness was something he could work on. Sure, it would take effort, but it couldn't be impossible.

Another thought crossed his mind – he should record this. Better still would be to see the film from the beginning. Flicking the information button, he was delighted to find he was watching the Sky Movies channel. There was a 'Plus One' channel just below it where the film hadn't started yet. He selected the new channel and set the Sky+ box to record the film.

'Perfect,' he breathed. 'Thanks, Jackie. I feel better already.'

He switched off the TV. Even with his bedroom door shut, he could smell that tea was nearly ready and the distant sounds of cutlery being put on the kitchen table gave fair warning that he would be called downstairs soon.

If I finish my maths homework quickly, there should be time to nip to the leisure centre after tea to see if there's a karate club here that I could try. If not, I could check online, but it would be good to go and see for myself.

Grabbing his schoolbag, he pulled out his maths book. Some of the pages were bent and a bit dirty after having been thrown in the mud earlier, but there wasn't much he could do about that. At least he hadn't lost the homework sheet. He scanned down the list of questions. They didn't look hard, but there were quite a lot of them. When the call came for tea, he'd almost done them all.

'Coming!' he called, placing his pen down on the book. It wouldn't take long to finish. He would eat tea even faster than usual, he decided. Despite still feeling a bit shaky after being caught by Zach and his gang, Donovan found he was surprisingly excited about his plan. Perhaps in a strange sort of way the bullies had done him a favour.

Chapter 3 – Allies

Going to the leisure centre to investigate had been a good idea, but now Donovan was faced with a tricky decision. Four different martial arts were available – none of them karate. There was a judo class running when he arrived, but after watching for a few minutes, Donovan could see it was a totally different fighting style to that of Jackie Chan. This left a choice between jado kuin do, tai chi and tae kwon do.

The easiest to cross off the list was tai chi. When he looked it up on the internet he found it was described as a 'soft martial art' that was mainly about balance and focus. Donovan couldn't see something like that scaring off Zach and his friends. Apparently jado kuin do and tae kwon do were both 'modern martial arts', developed in recent years by mixing together several different ancient martial arts to form a new fighting system. From what he could find on the internet, jado kuin do was a localised martial art with a small following. Tae kwon do had been around longer and was much more popular. A Korean General had invented it to train soldiers in the South Korean

Army – just what he needed. It was also an Olympic sport, which was amazing, given its short history. Both clubs offered a free first lesson, but on discovering one of the main roots of tae kwon do was karate, Donovan made the decision to try the Korean martial art.

Walking to school the next morning, his head was full of the spinning kicks and lightning fast punches.

'Hello, Donovan.'

He jumped. He had been so caught up in his daydream that he'd not noticed Gurveer step alongside him. There was a high-pitched giggle from behind.

'Hi, Gurveer,' he replied, glancing over his shoulder to find the source of the laughter. Two girls were following them. One he recognised as Gurveer's sister who was in the year below them. The other girl he had seen in the playground, but he didn't know her name. The two had their heads together and were whispering.

'So how are you enjoying Oxtree?' Gurveer asked, moving alongside him.

Great! Donovan thought. *How can I get rid of him? The last thing I need is to be seen hanging out with Gurveer.*

'It's OK, I s'pose,' he replied.

'One of the kids told me you sound like an owl.'

Donovan looked across at him, confused. 'Who?' he asked.

Gurveer laughed. 'Works every time,' he said with a grin.

Donovan groaned as he realised what he had just said. 'Are all your jokes that bad?'

'Pretty much,' he said with a shrug. 'The cornier the better I reckon. Zach and his friends seem to be giving you a hard time,' Gurveer added. 'They were picking on me before you came along, so I should thank you for taking their attention away.'

'They're a pain,' he said, looking down at the

pavement and trying to forget the incident in the park. 'But I can handle them.'

'You can?' Gurveer asked, clearly surprised. 'How?'

'Well... OK, I can't just yet,' he admitted. 'But I have a plan.'

'Really? What sort of plan?'

Donovan thought for a moment before answering. This wasn't the first time that Gurveer had taken time to greet him and be friendly. So far he had kept his distance, avoiding the offer of friendship for fear of losing his chance to get in with the popular kids. Donovan had never managed to make it into the 'in crowd' in his last school. He knew he was being selfish, but he had so wanted things to be different this time. It wasn't going to happen now. He could see that. Given what had happened after school yesterday, he realised that he would be foolish to push Gurveer away. He needed a friend.. A thought struck him.

'Gurveer, have you ever thought about learning self-defence?'

'What? Like kung fu, or something?'

'That sort of thing, yeah,' he said. 'I'm going to try a free taster lesson tonight at the leisure centre. It's not kung fu, though. It's tae kwon do. Fancy coming along?'

Gurveer thought for a moment. 'To be honest I'll never be a fighter,' he said. 'As my dad would say: I've got about as much speed and coordination as a slug that's been half-drowned in a saucer of beer. Even my sister is stronger than me.'

Donovan laughed. 'Oh come on! You can't be that bad. I'm no Jackie Chan either, but I want to see what it's like. Who knows? It could be fun.'

'It's free, is it?' Gurveer asked, pausing for a moment to consider. 'OK then. Why not? I'll have to get permission from my dad first, but it should be all right. What time?'

'Six 'til seven. '

'I'll ask as soon as I get home. You going on your bike?'

'Yep.'

'You live on the new estate, right?'

'That's right.'

'So you'll have to come down Station Road on the way to the leisure centre. We live at number fifty-eight.'

Donovan nodded. 'I'll find it. Meet you at about five thirty, OK?'

'Sure,' Gurveer looked across at Donovan. 'So this tae kwon do thing – is this your plan to deal with Zach?'

Donovan grinned. 'Sort of,' he admitted. 'I hope the instructors are good, because I've never been much good at sports.'

'You don't think the people there will turn out to be

like Zach and his friends, do you?' Gurveer asked with a note of concern in his voice. 'It's just that I don't need any more bullies in my life right now.'

'I doubt it,' Donovan replied. 'The classes are supposed to build confidence and I don't see how they're supposed to do that if the teachers or the senior students beat you up. I'm sure it'll be fine. We'll do it together – allies, right?'

'Allies?'

'Sure,' he said. 'Friends – allies – like the countries in World War II that came together to fight for the good of the world.'

'Allies. I like the sound of that.'

'You'll need to get your dad to sign a form for you. You can get one from the club website. Will he be OK with that?'

'Don't know until I try,' Gurveer said with a shrug. 'It should be OK though. He's always wanted me to take more of an interest in sports. I'll see you later.'

All through the day doubts niggled in Donovan's mind. Was he leading Gurveer into a situation that might get both of them hurt? On the plus side he managed to avoid Zach and his gang at lunchtime by going to art club in the library, and again after school by racing out as soon as the bell went. However, while the tactic had worked this time, he knew he couldn't keep hiding and running forever.

To his horror when he approached his mum with

the form for her to sign, she was not keen. He was so pleased that he had arranged to go with Gurveer and had promised to meet him, as this proved to be the deciding factor in getting her to agree.

'I can't let him down, mum!' he insisted. 'I promised I'd be there.'

'Well in future, don't make promises without checking with me first,' she replied. 'I would much prefer to see this class for myself before letting you try it, but the gas man is due here any minute to check out the boiler and dad's not going to be home until at least six. As you're going with a friend, I'll let you go this once. Take your phone and make sure you're back by six-thirty.'

'Yes, mum.'

When the time came to leave for the leisure centre that evening he realised that if he hadn't arranged for Gurveer to go with him, not only was it unlikely that his mum would have let him go, but he might have chickened out. Nervous as he was about the class, he was going to have to face Zach again at some point, so he might as well be as ready as possible.

It was good that he'd come to this conclusion, because when he reached Gurveer's house there was a surprise waiting for him.

Chapter 4 – First Lesson

'Hi, Gurveer. Ready?'

Although he was dressed in blue track suit bottoms and a sweatshirt, he looked far from ready. He was rubbing his hands together nervously and looking rather sheepish.

'Um... well... yes. Sort of,' he mumbled.

'What's the matter? Nervous?' Donovan asked, trying to hide his own worry behind a wide grin.

'No... er... well, yes... but that's not it,' Gurveer spluttered. 'It's just that dad wouldn't let me go unless... unless...'

'Unless he took me along,' said a confident girl's voice from behind the shelves. Gurveer's sister appeared at the far end of the hallway. Her dark brown eyes sparkled with amusement, and her lips were curled in a broad grin as she noted her brother's embarrassment. She was followed by her dark-haired friend. 'And I asked Gabriella to keep me company. I hope you don't mind us coming.'

Gabriella put a hand to her mouth and giggled.

Inside Donovan groaned. Giggling girls had

definitely not been a part of his plan, but he did his best not to show his feelings. He glanced at Gurveer who shrugged an apology.

'If that's what your dad said, then it's fine with me,' Donovan told them, giving the best smile he could muster. Although he was gritting his teeth at this turn of events, he had been brought up to be polite. 'Sorry, I know you're Gurveer's sister, but I don't know your name.'

'I'm Abi,' she replied. 'It's short for Abhaya. And

Gabriella is normally called Gabby, but Gabby and Abi makes us sound like wannabe twins, so when she's with me, I call her Gee. Isn't that right Gee?'

Gabriella nodded and giggled again.

'Fair enough – Abi and Gee. I can remember that.' He glanced at his watch. 'I'm Donovan, but I guess you know that already. Come on then. If you're coming, let's go. We don't want to be late.'

Once they were outside and on their bikes, Donovan rode alongside Gurveer with the girls following along behind. He tried to forget they were there, but it was hard to ignore their excited chattering voices and loud giggles. Gurveer pedalled along firing off one corny joke after another.

'What's white and can't climb trees?'

Donovan played along, glad of the distraction. 'I don't know. What's white and can't climb trees?'

'A fridge.'

Donovan groaned, but Gurveer just smiled and launched straight into the next one.

'Two snowmen are standing next to each other in a garden. One turns to the other and says "That's funny. I can smell carrots too!"'

Donovan was already wondering if inviting him along had been a mistake. Why hadn't he just gone alone? The girls were sure to embarrass them when they got there.

Arriving at the leisure centre the four chained their

bikes to the railings outside and entered through the automatic doors into the foyer. A figure in an all-black martial arts suit, tied at the waist with a black belt, was standing in the doorway to the gymnasium. On seeing him, Gurveer's stream of bad jokes stopped and he became suddenly quiet. The word 'Instructor' was stitched in small gold lettering on the right side of the man's chest and there were three thin golden stripes across the end of his black belt. He looked oriental;

medium height for a man and slim, with short-cropped hair. Donovan stared at him for a moment, trying to guess the man's age, but he found it impossible to judge. As the four approached him the instructor gave them a curious look before smiling.

'Are you coming to train with us?' he asked, tipping his head slightly to one side.

'Yes, sir,' Donovan replied. 'Your advert says you offer a free taster session.'

'We do. But I'm afraid that I'm going to have to get one of your parents to sign a form before I can take you on to the training floor,' he said, looking apologetic.

'I downloaded the form from your website and got my mum to sign it,' Donovan explained. 'Is this OK?'

The man took his form and checked it over carefully. 'This will be fine for tonight,' he said. 'And the rest of you?'

The children each pulled a folded sheet of paper from a pocket and passed it to him. He nodded, pleased.

'I will need to meet your parents and give them more paperwork if you are going to do more than a taster session.'

'We understand,' Donovan replied, glancing round at the others to check they were happy with him speaking for them. They seemed grateful.

'Good. Then welcome. I'm Kai Green, the senior

instructor here. Please stand straight and bow as you enter the training hall. Respect is one of the key teachings of tae kwon do. I'll see you inside in just a minute.'

The four entered the gym, each pausing in turn and bowing slightly as they entered through the door. Inside they saw about twenty people, a mixture of adults and children, chatting in small groups, stretching, jogging on the spot, or punching and kicking at imaginary opponents. Although some were practising fighting techniques, none of the people looked mean or nasty. Also, a lot were smiling and laughing – especially the younger ones, which made Donovan feel less nervous.

Moments later the instructor stepped in through the door behind them and the room fell silent. Many of the students stood to attention like soldiers.

'You four beginners, come over here next to me for a minute. The rest of you start running round the gym. Go!'

'Yes, sir!' the students chorused in response.

'OK,' he said giving them a friendly smile. 'Have any of you done any martial arts training before?'

They all shook their heads.

'Gabriella, I see from your form that you suffer from occasional asthma. Do you have an inhaler, or any medication with you?'

'No ... sir,' she replied hesitantly. 'I don't get it very

often. I should be fine.'

'All right,' he nodded. 'But if you do start to feel any ill effects, please let me know and feel free to move to the side and sit out at any time. Now, this first part of the class is a warm up, so copy the others as best you can and don't worry if you struggle with some of the exercises. No one will expect you to be perfect on the first night. Take your shoes and socks off. You can leave them here next to the wall. Then go and join the others in running round the gym and listen for my instructions.'

'Yes, sir,' Donovan said. The others repeated the formal reply and within seconds the four were running at a fast jog to keep up with the other students.

'I bought a racing snail the other day that can run nearly as fast as this,' Gurveer puffed, keeping his voice low to avoid drawing Kai's attention.

'Hmm,' Donovan replied, concentrating on his breathing and waiting for the punch line.

'Thought I'd try taking its shell off to see if it could go even faster.'

'And?' Donovan asked, unable to resist.

'It didn't work,' Gurveer replied, giving him a wide grin. 'It just made the poor thing more sluggish. More sluggish... get it?'

Donovan groaned and shook his head. 'They get worse!' he said.

For the next ten minutes the instructor directed

them through a mixture of exercises. They started by running for a few minutes before stopping and doing a series of strength-building exercises. The warm-up finished with some difficult stretches. Donovan glanced across with envy as Gabriella made each of them look easy. When Kai asked the class to stand with their legs as wide apart as possible, she was able to drop easily all the way down until her bottom was on the floor and her legs out to either side of her body. ..

'Very good, Gabriella!' Kai said, with a smile. 'Have you done gymnastics by any chance?'

'Five years of ballet,' she replied.

He nodded. 'You can stretch much further than most of my students. This will help a lot with some of the things I will teach you in tae kwon do.'

Next it was into lines like military ranks with the senior students to the front, moving down through the grades to the four beginners at the back. The senior black belt called the class to attention and then everyone bowed to the instructor before the formal part of the lesson began. Kai handed over the main class to one of his assistants and called Donovan, Gurveer, Abi and Gabriella to one side, where he began to teach them how to stand properly and how to throw a powerful punch.

Donovan concentrated fiercely throughout the lesson. Although Kai called the commands in Korean, he repeated them in English for the beginners and

Donovan found he quickly picked up many of the basic terms. Many times he found himself getting angry with himself, as his body didn't seem to want to do what his mind was telling it. *This should be easy!* he thought. But it wasn't.

For most of the lesson he stepped forwards and backwards trying to do what Kai called an obverse punch. This was a punch with the same arm as the leg he had forward. It felt wrong. No matter how hard he tried, he could not seem to throw his fist with any real power.

'Relax, Donovan!' Kai told him for what must have been the tenth time. 'You're trying too hard. Relax. Start the punch slowly and snap it out at the end. Focus on the target point. I know it feels unnatural. Here, watch again.'

Kai showed him the move again. Stepping forwards his arm shot out so fast that the loose material on the arm of his training suit made a snapping sound like a whip-crack. Donovan sighed. *If only,* he thought. *I'll never be able to punch that hard.*

'If only the punch lines of your jokes were that sharp, Gurveer,' he muttered to his friend. 'You might get a few more laughs.'

'Ha, ha!' he replied softly, shooting out a punch with more power.

'Good, Gurveer,' Kai praised instantly. 'That's much better. Well done. Good effort. I know it might seem boring to spend the entire lesson doing just these basic moves, but if you're serious about learning tae kwon do, you'll find there's a lot of repetition to begin with. To get to any real standard takes years of practice. Relax for a moment – all of you. Take a seat on the bench there.'

Kai turned and pointed to one of the other black belts. 'Pad up, Wayne,' he called. 'I want to show these kids what they're working towards.'

Chapter 5 – The Uncomfortable Truth

'Cheryots! Kyung ye. Chunbi. Free spar at my command. Light contact only. Seejak!'

Donovan's eyes opened wide and his jaw dropped. 'Wow!' he breathed.

'Cool!' Gurveer murmured at the same time.

With the courtesies of standing to attention and bowing to one another complete, the two black belts, Kai and Wayne, both adopted a fighting guard position at the order *Chunbi* and sprang into action at the command *Seejak*. They were fast – lightning fast! Hands and feet flashed in a whirling dance, searching for gaps in their opponent's defence.

After nearly forty-five minutes of being taught how to stand correctly, how to make a proper fist, and how to step forwards and backwards while trying to throw punches that Kai would be happy with, Donovan had begun to wonder if he had made a mistake by coming to this class. It was not what he had imagined at all. Now, watching the two black belts sparring, he realised that he had come to the right place after all.

He wanted to be able to move like these two men.

Both Kai and Wayne seemed to possess a sixth sense, avoiding or blocking the other's attacks again and again. And when one did land a blow with fist or foot, it was obvious by the sound of the impact that the attacker had controlled the power of the technique so well that it made contact with only the lightest of touches. Without pin-point control, any one of those kicks or punches could easily have been delivered with bone-crunching power. It was amazing to watch. They were like two deadly ballet dancers; balanced and light on their feet, incredibly flexible and oh, so quick!

‘I don’t think I could ever be that fast!’ Donovan whispered to Gurveer.

‘You never know unless you try,’ he replied. ‘And I really want to try.’

Donovan looked at Gurveer. The boy’s face was set with determination. ‘I believe you,’ he said. ‘And I’m going to be right there trying with you.’

‘Barrol!’ Kai’s order ended the fight. Both men were breathing hard and smiling. ‘Cheryots! Kyung ye.’ They stood to attention and bowed to each other again.

There seemed to be a lot of bowing going on, Donovan decided. Was all that really necessary? It seemed crazy to bow to your opponent before trying to hit them.

‘That’s what you’ll be working up towards,’ Kai told them, still grinning and panting slightly as he removed his padded head guard and wiped the sweat from his forehead with his sleeve. ‘What do you think? Are you still interested?’

‘Definitely!’

‘Absolutely!’

‘Yes.’

‘Yes.’

There was no hesitation from any of them. All four answered together as one.

‘That’s great,’ Kai said, nodding. Then his face turned serious. ‘But before I agree to teach you, I want you to consider why you want to learn.' He looked Donovan directly in the eyes. 'If you think I'm going to teach you just so you can fight someone who's bothering you, you can think again.'

Donovan shifted uncomfortably, feeling the heat rising into his cheeks. Did Kai know what he had been thinking? Could he tell that Donovan had been bullied just by looking at him?

'There is no hiding that tae kwon do skills can be used as a weapon,' he continued. 'The knowledge of this martial art in the wrong hands can be every bit as lethal as giving someone a loaded gun. This is why you must have a license to practise the art. Abuse the skills we teach and you will not only be in a lot of trouble, but your license will be taken away and you will never be allowed to train with others again.'

'But tae kwon do is for self-defence, isn't it... sir?' Gurveer asked, almost forgetting the formality of calling the instructor 'sir'.

'Yes, but only as a last resort,' Kai replied, switching his intense gaze to the other boy. 'And even then, you should only use the minimum force needed to get out of the situation. Where at all possible, you should look to avoid situations that might lead to fights outside of the dojang. I won't lie to you. A martial art is not a magic shield. No matter how good you get at the art of tae kwon do, there will always be situations that are beyond your skill level to fight your way out from. If

you find yourself facing a possible fight and you have the opportunity to run away, you should do so. What you will learn here will help you realise this truth.'

'Sir, I don't want to fight anyone,' Abi said carefully. 'But I can see how learning to defend myself could be useful. My mum and dad seemed pleased that I wanted to learn how to do this. Surely fighting other people is what martial arts are all about, isn't it?'

'On one level, you're quite right,' Kai agreed. 'When General Choi Hong Hi of the Korean Army developed this martial art, he said this knowledge would allow the weak to have a fine weapon to defend themselves with. But he didn't just see tae kwon do as a weapon. He saw it as a way of life that would help make the student a better person. Tae kwon do is built on the pillars of being polite, being truthful, not giving up no matter how hard it gets, whilst showing self-control and an unbreakable spirit. A student should be humble, loyal and dedicated. It is not an easy path to take. I don't expect you to remember these things now, but I want you to think carefully about why you want to learn before before coming back to class next week.'

'Yes, sir,' Abi replied.

The others echoed her with meek voices.

'So he'll teach us how to fight if we promise to run away at the first sign of trouble?' Donovan muttered angrily as they unlocked their bikes from the railings. 'I bet Zach'll just love rubbing my nose in that if he finds out!'

'So don't tell him,' Abi said. 'Kai's right. Fighting Zach will only land you in a whole load of trouble anyway. Let the teachers deal with Zach.'

'What? Like they have so far, you mean?'

'Did you tell the teachers what Zach has been doing?' Gabriella asked.

Donovan swung his leg over the saddle and gripped the handlebars fiercely. 'No,' he muttered.

‘Well, you can hardly blame them for not doing anything then,’ she said, and with that she pushed off and pedalled away on to the road with Abi close behind her.

‘Girls!’ Gurveer said with a shrug. ‘They never understand.’

Donovan wanted to agree. He didn’t want the other kids to see him hiding behind the teachers all the time. That was as good as wearing a sign around his neck that read, “I’m weak. Pick on me!” But as much as he wanted to ignore her comments, he could not shake the uncomfortable feeling that Gabriella might be right.

Pushing off from the kerb, Donovan tried to get Gabriella’s words out of his mind. As they rode away, neither he nor Gurveer noticed the figure watching them from behind the tinted windscreen of his car across the road.

Chapter 6 – Trouble

'I'm sorry, Donovan. It's too expensive. I talked it over with your father last night and we simply can't afford it.'

Donovan's heart sank. He knew that tone. It was final. There was no arguing with Mum when she used that voice. And just like that his dreams of learning a martial art were crushed.

'Can't I at least talk to him about it? I'd give up my pocket money and take a paper round and...'

'It's thirty-five pounds just for the license,' she sighed, pointing at the information sheet Kai had given him. 'Then there's the cost of the suit and the monthly training fees, and that's before you add in the cost of the exams. And, knowing you, you'd want to enter competitions as well. No, Donovan. It's too much. You're welcome to talk to your dad when he gets home tonight if you like, but you'll get the same answer from him. If we had that sort of money to spend on your hobbies, I'd be happy to pay it, but we haven't. We're stretched to the limit just paying the bills. Why don't you see if you can find something a little less expensive to do with your spare time?'

'This isn't just a hobby,' he grumbled. 'It's self-defence. I thought you'd want me to be able to defend myself.'

'Don't take that tone with me, young man!' she snapped, turning and glaring at him with hard eyes. 'Go to your room right now! I've said no and that's the end of it. Dinner will be in about twenty minutes. You can come back down and apologise then.'

Donovan didn't reply. He was too angry. But what could he do? He stamped up the stairs and slammed his bedroom door shut. No doubt he would be in further trouble for that, but he didn't care. The ironic thing was that the reason he wanted to learn tae kwon do was because Zach and his gang of bullies thought he was from a wealthy family. He didn't know whether to laugh at that thought, or cry. It seemed his lifeline had been cut before he had even begun to pull himself to safety.

* * * * *

'Master?'

The room was lit only by a half dozen flickering candles. In the centre of the floor sat the hunched figure of the Master wrapped in a dark hooded cloak before the bronze statue of a rearing cobra. The light from the candles cast several shadows of the snake on to the far wall that appeared to dance and sway with every slight movement of the flames.

'You know better than to disturb me when I'm meditating, Driss,' the man said softly. 'This had better be important.'

How did he know who it was, without looking? Driss wondered. *It could have been any one of the Master's employees.* A cold, invisible hand of fear seemed to reach into his chest and squeeze his heart.

'I apologise, Master,' he stammered. 'But I thought this news was too important to wait. Kai gained four new students this evening.'

'Four? You're sure of this? And they arrived together?'

'Yes, Master.'

'It's too early,' he muttered. 'We're not ready yet. But it might not be them. It doesn't have to be them.'

'Your orders, Master?'

The figure on the floor did not answer. The silence stretched as Driss waited, watching as his master sat quietly thinking. It was hot in the room; unnaturally hot considering the only apparent source of heat was the six candles. Driss felt the first beads of sweat break out across his forehead.

'What are they like, these students? Do they appear to be the warriors foretold?'

Driss jumped at the sudden question.

'In truth, Master – no. They looked like ordinary children to me, but you said ...'

'Children?'

'Yes, Master.'

There was a short pause and then the cloaked figure began to chuckle, his voice low and deep. The sound sent a chill through Driss.

'You came to tell me about a group of children?'

'But, Master, you said ...'

'Warn me if Kai should take on four new students,'

the figure finished. 'Yes. Yes, I did. And you have done as I bid. Thank you, Driss.'

'So what would you have me do, Master?'

'Continue to watch Kai. It wouldn't hurt to watch these children too. And if they display any signs of being ... special, I will deal with them. Otherwise, do not draw attention to yourself. Watch. Listen. Report to me. That is all.'

'Yes, Master.'

* * * * *

'So what've you got for me today, posh boy?'

Shock and fear gripped Donovan. He turned to run, but two of Zach's gang had appeared on the path behind him. How could he have been so careless? He had been daydreaming – thinking of endless unlikely plans for raising enough money to train at tae kwon do without the help of his parents. He had not been thinking about where he was going as he entered the alleyway. He felt sick inside. *Stupid! Stupid! STUPID!* he thought. There was no way out of here except past Zach and his gang. The walls on either side of the alley were too high to scale. Zach had picked his spot well.

'Not a lot,' Donovan shrugged, trying to stay calm. 'I'm guessing it's my money you want. Here – take it.'

He fished round in his pockets and pulled out the three pounds he had there.

'See boys, I told you he was smart,' Zach said, flashing a nasty grin.

'He's probably trying to avoid another wedgie,' one of the other boys laughed.

'More'n likely,' Zach agreed. 'He did look a little uncomfortable after the last one. Three quid, eh? Well, that's slightly better, I s'pose. What's in your lunch box today? Anything worth having?'

There was a chuckle from the boys closing in behind Donovan. 'I'm sure you'll find something, Zach. You seem to like most food.'

'Shut it, Marcus,' Zach barked, but the other boys laughed and Zach was forced to laugh with them to save face. 'What can I say? I'm a growing lad, OK?' he said with a shrug.

Growing yes – growing outwards, Donovan thought, but he said nothing as he pulled out his lunch box from his backpack and handed that over too. *Oh, how I'd love to wipe that smile off your face by planting my foot in it!*

Zach opened the lid and threw it over his shoulder. He sniffed at the sandwiches.

'Tuna? Yuck!' Zach threw them high over the wall at the side of the alley, much to the amusement of the other boys. Donovan said nothing. He stood in silence and watched as Zach pocketed his crisps and chocolate bar before emptying his drink bottle on to the pavement.

'Thanks for not a lot, posh boy,' Zach sneered, dropping the lunch box and turning to leave. 'Tell your mum you don't want fish any more, got it?'

Donovan said nothing.

One of the other boys shoved him from behind. 'Zach asked you a question.'

'I heard him,' Donovan muttered.

'Good. Better do as he says then,' the boy warned, walking past to join the others. 'Unless you like having your pants pulled up round your ears, of course.'

The gang laughed again, leaving him to gather the empty bits of his lunch box and put them back into his backpack. He felt hungry already. Hungry and very, *very* angry.

Chapter 7 – Lucky Break

Donovan sat in his room sulking. He glanced over at his alarm clock and clenched his fists as he saw the time. Gurveer, Abi and Gee would be arriving at the leisure centre for their second lesson with Kai any time now. It wasn't fair. When they had moved here, it had been because his dad had been offered a better job, paying more money. At no time had mum or dad said anything about spending all of this extra money and more on getting a bigger house. It seemed like they were worse off now than they had been before dad got his promotion.

Downstairs the phone began to ring. He heard his mother answer it.

'Hello, six four five one double five,' she said, almost singing the numbers. 'Yes, that's right... Really? No! Why that's fantastic! ...Yes, of course. I'll run him down there right now. See you in a few minutes. Thank you *so* much for ringing. Bye.'

Donovan could not help being just a little curious to know what his mother was so enthusiastic about. He could hear her coming up the stairs. When she knocked and entered his room her face was beaming.

'You're never going to guess what?' she said.

'Dad's got another promotion and we're moving again?' Donovan replied, thinking back to the last time he had seen her so happy.

'No,' she said. 'I have a feeling you're going to think this is much better news than that. It seems that someone somewhere is looking out for you. That was the instructor from the tae kwon do school, Kai is it?'

'That's right,' Donovan said, his heart beginning to race. Had his mum decided to let him learn after all?

'It seems you were the one thousandth person to fill in an application form for a license with his club since he began teaching and he has decided to use the occasion to gain some publicity. He's offering you a whole year of free training – license and everything in return for our allowing a photo of you to appear in the local paper with an article about the club and how he's given you this free scholarship. Apparently we will still have to buy a suit and pay for any exams you take, but if you're willing to put your pocket money towards it, then I think our budget might just run to that.'

'YES!' he shouted, punching the air with delight.

'Anyway, Kai was ringing to see if you were on your way and I said I'd run you over there, so you'd better get changed quickly.'

'Go start the car, Mum. I'll be there in thirty seconds.'

Donovan was true to his word, throwing off his clothes and putting on his tracksuit bottoms, T-shirt and trainers in record time. He hurtled down the stairs, taking them three at a time. Within another two minutes they were pulling into the leisure centre car park, and two minutes after that he was running round the gym with his friends feeling happier than he'd felt all week.

'It's good that you could make it,' Gurveer said to him softly as they lapped the gym for the second time. 'I didn't really fancy doing this with just the girls for company.'

'Worried they would show you up?'

Gurveer grinned. 'Something like that,' he replied.

'Stop chatting boys and concentrate on what you're doing. Everyone down, ten press ups – Donovan it's your count.'

'One... two... three...' Donovan called, counting with each repeated exercise. He tried to make his press ups good ones, as he felt like all eyes in the hall were on him.

The class was tougher this time. Kai pushed them hard, both during the warm up and the teaching phase, but Donovan didn't mind one bit. He loved every second of the lesson and tried his best at everything Kai showed them.

As before, Abi and Gee both found the stretching exercises easier than the boys. They also kicked higher and with more balance, winning Kai's approval each time. But when it came to punching, it was Donovan who shone. He had been practising in front of the mirror in his room every night since the last lesson, watching to make sure his fist was correctly formed and that his punches came from the hip, just the way Kai had taught them.

'Very good, Donovan. *Very* good! You've been practising.'

'Yes, sir,' he replied.

'It shows. Now let's see how you do with the movement exercises we did last week.'

By the end of the lesson Donovan could feel where he was going to hurt in the morning. Some of the stretching exercises Kai had shown them had pulled on muscles he didn't know were there, and the repeated tensing and relaxing of muscles as he punched and blocked had made his shoulders and back ache. He knew he would be sore, but he didn't care.

Before leaving the hall at the end of the class he approached Kai, stood to attention and bowed.

'Thank you, sir,' he said.

Kai returned the bow and gave him a warm smile.

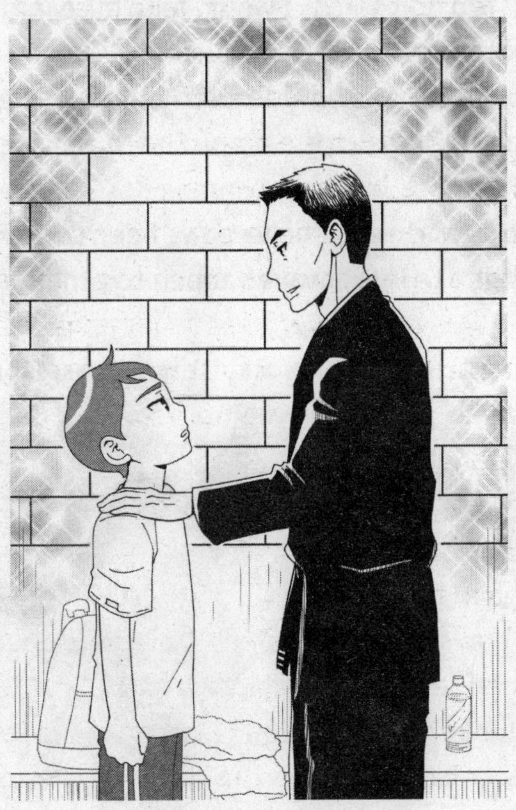

'My pleasure,' he replied. 'Now we must arrange a photo for the paper and I'll need to write down a few details for the news article.'

'Sir?'

'Yes, Donovan?'

'Am I really your one thousandth student here?' he asked, keeping his voice low to avoid anyone else hearing.

'Of course,' Kai said, a sparkle dancing in his eyes as he said it. 'Otherwise how could I write the news article? You don't think I would feed false information to our local newspaper, do you?'

'No, sir,' he answered quickly, hoping he hadn't offended his instructor. 'It's just ...'

'Just ... ?'

'Nothing, sir. I can't believe I've been so lucky, that's all. Things like this always happen to other kids – not me.'

'Well everyone gets lucky sometimes, Donovan – even you.'

Chapter 8 – Bad Decision

'Go outside and get some fresh air, boys.'

'But, Miss Borland, Mr Hedges said Gurveer and me could ...'

'That's Gurveer and I,' the teacher corrected, giving Donovan a cold stare. 'And I don't care what Mr Hedges said. It's a beautiful day out there. I'm not going to have you skulking round the cloakroom at lunchtime when the sun is shining. No excuses. Go outside and play. Now!'

'Yes, Miss,' the boys grumbled, turning towards the door.

'Just our luck to get caught by boring Borland,' Gurveer muttered as they stepped outside. 'I bet nobody picked on her when she was at school. I couldn't even imagine Zach taking her on.'

'Nor me,' Donovan agreed. 'If she didn't zap him with her laser eyes, she'd bore him to death.'

The two boys laughed, but the momentary good mood was short-lived. As they moved out on to the playground Donovan looked round for Zach. He was at the far end of the tarmac with his gang. They were kicking a ball around, but as soon as Zach noticed Donovan he stopped. He looked like a cat that had spotted prey and if Zach's ears could have pricked up, they would have. The rest of his gang slowly noticed their leader's focus and turned one by one. Donovan froze like a rabbit caught in a spotlight, his heart suddenly pounding.

'I've got a bad feeling about this,' Gurveer said nervously.

'You've watched Star Wars too many times,' Donovan replied, keeping his eyes locked firmly on Zach and trying to ignore his fear. 'Next you'll be saying *Look at the size of that thing!*'

'I was actually thinking of a different quote.'

'Really? Which quote was that?'

'The one where Han Solo yells *RUN!*'

'Yes, but where to?' Donovan asked, panic rising as he looked round for an escape route. 'There's nowhere to hide out here. Where's the lunchtime supervisor?'

'Over there by the benches,' Gurveer replied. 'It looks like one of the reception kids has fallen over and cut her knee. The teacher's comforting her. Look!'

'Maybe she could do with some help,' Donovan suggested.

'Good idea. Let's go and ...'

But it was already too late. Zach had noticed where the boys' eyes had drifted and had sent two of his gang ahead to cut them off from reaching the teacher.

Worse, the teacher looked as if she was about to take the little girl inside through the door by the staff room. Zach had clearly noticed this and was signalling the rest of his gang to spread out and start forwards.

The net was closing. Donovan hesitated, unsure if it was better to try to run and dodge the gang for as long as possible, or to let them come to him here in the open. Neither option seemed likely to end well.

'If we run, it'll look like we're playing some sort of game,' Donovan muttered. 'That'll just make it easier for them to take us down. Let's stand our ground.'

'Are you sure?' Gurveer asked. He sounded terrified.

'No,' he admitted. 'But I can't keep running from Zach forever.'

'I can.'

'Then go ahead, but I'm staying here.'

Gurveer didn't move. Donovan was relieved. It would have been harder without Gurveer next to him, but he had made up his mind. Zach had forced his hand. He would not run this time. He could feel his friend's fear, and out of the corner of his eye he could see the boy's hands shaking. Zach and three of his gang approached, spread out in a closing semi-circle. The bully had a sneering grin on his face.

'Not giving us the sport of catching you today, posh boy? I'm disappointed,' Zach jeered.

'I'm sorry,' Donovan replied quietly. 'I didn't realise I was ruining your fun, but I'm done with running from you.'

'Good. That will make life easier. Now hand it over.'

'Hand what over?'

'Your money, of course.'

'No.'

Zach's eyes widened slightly. 'What did you say?' he asked, his voice low and dangerous.

'I said no. You're not getting my money,' Donovan repeated.

Zach had a quick scan round the playground to

make sure the teacher had not reappeared. She hadn't.

'I guess it's wedgie time then. Grab them, boys!'

'Low block, Gurveer – NOW!' Donovan ordered. 'KEEEAAAHHH!'

As one he and Gurveer stepped back into walking stance and snapped their left arms downwards to stop about a fist-width above their left knees. Zach and his gang stopped. For a moment they looked unsure. Zach looked round again for the teacher. The shout that the two boys had let out had been very loud, but there was still no sign of any adults.

'So the geeks have started karate lessons,' Zach sneered. 'I see they taught you how to shout. Very impressive, I'm sure.'

As Zach moved forwards again, Donovan suddenly knew what he had to do. Clenching his fists really tight he took a long step forwards, closing the distance between him and Zach. Everything seemed to happen in slow motion as he concentrated on what Kai had taught him.

'Donovan ... NO!' Gurveer yelled, but his shout had not even ended before it was all over.

Focusing all his energy, Donovan drove his right fist forwards while pulling back his left to generate extra reaction force. It hammered into Zach's stomach with a satisfying thud, hitting just under the boy's rib cage. The big lad gave a 'whoof!' of surprise and doubled over, all the breath driven from his lungs. Donovan pulled straight back into walking stance again, alert and ready to block if any of the other boys attacked.

An instant later a loud whistle blast drew everyone's attention.

'DONOVAN RICHARDS! Come here this instant!'

It was Miss Borland. Her laser eyes looked to be set at full power. Donovan could feel the heat of them from halfway across the playground and he felt his cheeks flush under their sizzling stare.

'Oh, poo!' Gurveer muttered. 'You're for it now!'

Donovan's heart sank. He didn't need Gurveer to tell him how much trouble he was in. He knew. He was up to his neck and sinking fast.

Chapter 9 – Warrior Kids

'You four – a word, please.'

Kai did not look happy. Donovan could guess why, but how had he found out? He led them to an empty room across the hall from the gym and closed the door behind him.

'Donovan, would you like to explain yourself?'

'Sir?' he asked. He turned momentarily away from his instructor, tugged nervously at the hem of his clean white training suit top, straightened his white belt and smoothed the material across his chest before turning back to face Kai's disapproving stare.

'Despite my warning when you started here a few weeks ago, I'm told you've been fighting.'

'It wasn't a fight, sir,' Gurveer said quickly. 'Donovan threw one punch, that's all.'

'One punch is all it takes,' Kai said, unimpressed. 'You could have seriously hurt that boy, Donovan. You realise that by all rights I should throw you out of the club here and now? Normally I wouldn't hesitate, but there are circumstances here that you're not aware of and I want to hear your side of the story before I make my decision.'

'But, sir...' Gurveer began.

'Enough from you, Gurveer. Your friend can speak for himself.'

'I was fed up with running, sir,' Donovan explained, unable to meet his instructor's eyes. He felt ashamed for breaking Kai's trust. 'Zach and his gang have been on my back ever since I moved here a couple of months ago. They've hurt me a couple of times and often steal my money and my lunch. I'm sorry, sir. I just wanted to warn him off, that's all.'

'So you hit him.'

'Zach and his gang were threatening us again. I thought I would get a shot in first this time.'

Kai sighed and put his hands on his hips.

'Hitting him was not the right thing to do, Donovan. You know that, don't you?'

'Yes, sir.'

'Did any of your teachers know you were being bullied?'

'No, sir.'

'Why didn't you tell them?'

'It ... it didn't feel ... right, sir,' Donovan said slowly, struggling to find the right words. 'I didn't want to get a name for telling tales. Nobody likes a tell-tale.'

Kai shook his head. 'You're right, Donovan – nobody likes tell-tales, but believe me – they like bullies even less. It takes courage to admit you're being bullied. Next time don't hide it. Tell one of the teachers, or tell me. Try Mr Hedges. I think you'll find he'll listen, and I certainly will.'

'You know our teachers?' Gurveer asked, surprised.

'Sit down,' Kai ordered. 'On the floor. Now – all of you.' He turned to the side and began pacing to and fro. For several seconds he remained silent. Then he stopped pacing and turned to face them.

Donovan sat and kept his eyes focused down at the floor.

'I probably shouldn't tell you this,' Kai began. 'But I think it might help if you knew why I have a special interest in teaching you four. I happen to think there is something unusual about you – all of you. I'm not sure quite what it is yet, but I mean to find out. So far you all show potential, but otherwise you're unremarkable students.'

'What makes you think we're unusual, sir?' Abi asked. 'I don't understand.'

'I'm not sure I do either, Abi,' he answered. 'But I'll try to explain. I don't know if what I'm about to tell you is nonsense, or the most important thing you'll ever hear, but it started before you were born. I was travelling in the Far East, searching for answers to some of life's more difficult questions. I spent much of my time meeting wise men and studying with any martial arts masters who would teach me. While there, I was accepted into training by one strange old

master who was respected by many for his wisdom. One night, after training with him for nearly a year, he told me he had seen something in my future – a vision. At first I thought he was crazy, but whenever I think of the look on the old man's face as he said it, I get a rash of goose bumps across my body. I have never been able to forget his words.'

He paused and looked at them. Donovan looked up. Kai appeared undecided on whether he should continue talking.

'Sir?' Donovan prompted, suddenly desperate to find out what the old man had predicted. 'What did this old master tell you?'

'He said that one day four young warriors would come to me for training,' Kai said, his face perfectly serious. 'That I must do anything in my power to help them, for they would face difficult and dangerous challenges that would affect the fate of many. Despite trying to leave the words behind, they haunt my dreams. In all the years since, I have never had four students begin training with me on the same day ... until you came along – four young warriors.'

'Warriors, sir?' Abi laughed. 'I don't think we qualify as warriors.'

'Really, Abi?' Kai asked, his mouth twisting into a smile. 'Your names suggest otherwise. I took the time to look them up. Donovan, yours is an old Irish name meaning *dark warrior*. Gurveer, your name means *warrior of the guru* and Gabriella means *warrior of God*.'

'But Abhaya doesn't mean warrior,' Abi said thoughtfully.

'No. You're right. It doesn't,' Kai agreed, nodding. 'Abhaya means *fearless*, but you also wrote your middle name on your application form. Luann is not a traditional Indian name, is it?'

'No,' Abi replied. 'Mum tells me it's a European

name, German I think, but she really liked it and she managed to convince Dad that a non-traditional middle name was not a bad thing.'

'Do you know the meaning of Luann?'

'Warrior?' she guessed.

'*Graceful warrior* to be exact,' he told her. 'So we have a dark warrior, a warrior of the guru, a warrior of God and a fearless, graceful warrior. Even if it's pure chance that you are all named for warriors, my instinct tells me otherwise. My old master made me swear to him that I would teach and protect the four young warriors until they were ready to face their destiny.'

'Wow!' Gurveer breathed.

'Well, look at me! I'm a warrior kid!' Gabriella giggled. 'Cool!'

'But I can't teach and protect you if you're going to start picking fights left, right and centre, can I, Donovan?'

Kai looked down and Donovan squirmed under his gaze. If anything Kai's eyes were even more fearsome than Miss Borland's.

'No, sir,' Donovan muttered. 'Sorry, sir.'

'For one thing, your school will ask me to expel you from the club if the teachers see you using your skills in the playground and I'll have no choice but to do as they ask, so keep it in the training hall. That goes for all of you, OK?'

'Yes, sir,' they chorused.

Donovan found Kai's story almost unbelievable. It sounded like the sort of thing that happened in books, or in films. Destiny? Difficult and dangerous challenges that would affect the lives of many – it all sounded very dramatic and mystical.

'Did your master tell you anything about these dangers we are supposed to face?' he asked thoughtfully.

'A little,' Kai admitted. 'But this is not the time to talk about that. We should be training. I'll tell you what I know when I think you're ready – not before. Now, let's get going. You need to warm up.'

Chapter 10 – STOP! THIEVES!

The four children were walking back from the leisure centre together after class and chatting about their lesson when it happened.

'STOP! THIEVES! COME BACK HERE!'

Even coming from inside the minimart the shop owner's angry voice was loud enough to echo down the street as Donovan saw three youths burst out through the doors. Without pausing to check it was clear, the three figures raced across the road and into the alleyway opposite.

'Come on, guys!' Gurveer urged. 'That's Mr Patchesa's shop. We should help. Those kids are no bigger than us.' He launched into a run. 'STOP! THIEVES!' he shouted, echoing the shop owner's words. as he sprinted after them.

'Gurveer! What do you think you're doing?' Donovan called after him, hesitant to follow. *Kai will be furious if we get into a fight,* he thought. *He'll kick us out of the club for sure.*

But Donovan couldn't let his friend risk chasing after three criminals alone. Well – not alone: Abi and Gee had already followed. Seeing them run after Gurveer gave him even more reason to join in. If the girls were brave enough to chase after the thieves and risk Kai's wrath, he wasn't ready to be left behind.

Mr Patchesa appeared in the doorway of the minimart.

'Don't worry, sir,' Donovan called out to him as he sprinted across the road. 'We'll get them for you. Call the police.'

Gurveer and the girls were in the alleyway ahead of him, but he wasn't far behind. Normally his lungs began to burn almost the moment he started to run, but not this time. He felt strong. Leaning forwards he accelerated, catching up first with the girls and then, having overtaken them as he ran through the alleyway, he caught up with Gurveer.

As they emerged from the alley side by side, Donovan realised the three thieves had split up.

'You go after that one,' Gurveer said, breathing hard and pointing. 'I'll take this one.'

'No!' Donovan replied. 'We stick together. If we get one, the police should be able to get the rest.'

'Make's sense,' Gurveer agreed, and they were running again, turning right to follow Gurveer's chosen target.

Gurveer had chosen well. The boy they were following was not a fast runner and Donovan could see that he was already struggling to keep going. Slowly but surely they were gaining on him. Donovan glanced over his shoulder to see if the girls were keeping up. They were.

The boy ahead reached the end of the street and was forced to pause a moment to wait for two cars to pass before he could cross the intersection. The brief stop made all the difference. Donovan and Gurveer were almost on him as he set off across the road and they caught him as he reached the pavement on the far side.

Realising he couldn't outrun his pursuers, the boy stopped and turned, lifting his hands as a sign of surrender.

'Please!' he begged, pulling back his hood. 'Don't hurt me! It wasn't my idea. I didn't take anything valuable. It was just a few sweets for a dare. Here. Take them. Just don't hurt me! Please!'

'Marcus?' Donovan said, surprised to see the boy from his school holding out a handful of chocolate bars in a trembling hand.

'I saw you hit Zach the other day, Donovan,' Marcus replied, his eyes darting from one white suit to the next as the four surrounded him. 'You really hurt him, you know. I'll come quietly, I promise. You don't need to hit me.'

'Was Zach one of the other two?' Gurveer asked, adopting a fighting stance, his right fist resting lightly against his cheek.

'N... n... no,' Marcus stammered. 'Not tonight.'

'But he has taken stuff in the past, hasn't he?'

Marcus gulped and nodded.

'I knew it!'

'Well I suggest you tell the police what you know,' Donovan said, trying to make his voice sound ominous. 'Mr Patchesa has called them. They won't be long. Come on. Lead the way back to the shop, Marcus. And let's avoid the alleys this time, shall we?'

As they walked back towards the minimart, Donovan realised this was the breakthrough he needed in dealing with Zach. The bully was going to be in a lot of trouble after the police talked to Marcus. The teachers would be watching Zach and his gang a lot more closely now, and were likely to believe Donovan if Zach started picking on him again. He hadn't needed to use his tae kwon do skills this evening, so Kai would have nothing to complain about. All in all things could not have worked out much better.

Gurveer was the best sort of friend he could imagine. He was brave and loyal, and they had the common interest of tae kwon do to enjoy together. Even Abi and Gee were not too bad to be around. Gee's giggling was irritating, but if Kai's story about the prophecy was true, then there must be more to her than just girly giggles. In just a few short weeks he had found his place in school. Zach was still likely to be a problem, but Donovan was no longer scared of him.

'Four young warriors,' he muttered. 'Warrior kids even! Maybe there is something special about us. Maybe...'

* * * * *

Driss was thoughtful as he watched the four children march their captive along the pavement back towards the minimart. Following them had not been easy, but

he had correctly guessed which way they would run and had been in the perfect position to observe the end of the chase.

His Master had been dismissive of the news that four children had begun studying with Kai, but perhaps this incident would make him think again. Driss waited patiently for them to pass by his car, confident they could not see him through the dark tinted windows. They looked so young. But even young people in the wrong place at the wrong time could potentially cause problems – especially if they had been trained by Kai.

'I think I'd better try to learn more about these kids,' he whispered to himself. 'Even if the Master isn't convinced, it wouldn't hurt to be forewarned. It's always good to be one step ahead of your enemy.'

Coming soon: Warrior Kids Book 2 – Pull no Punches!
www.markrobsonauthor.com